GRANDPA'S SONG

TONY JOHNSTON · *pictures by* BRAD SNEED

DIAL BOOKS FOR YOUNG READERS NEW YORK

Published by Dial Books for Young Readers
A Division of Penguin Books USA Inc.
375 Hudson Street
New York, New York 10014

Printed in Hong Kong by South China Printing Company (1988) Limited
Design by Atha Tehon
First Edition
1 3 5 7 9 10 8 6 4 2

Library of Congress Cataloging in Publication Data
Johnston, Tony.
Grandpa's song / by Tony Johnston ; pictures by Brad Sneed.
p.   cm.
Summary: When a young girl's beloved, exuberant grandfather
becomes forgetful, she helps him by singing their favorite song.
ISBN 0-8037-0801-7.—ISBN 0-8037-0802-5 (lib. bdg.)
[1. Grandfathers—Fiction. 2. Singing—Fiction. 3. Old age—Fiction.]
I. Sneed, Brad, ill. II. Title.
PZ7.J6478Gr   1991   [E]—dc20
90-43836   CIP   AC

The art for each picture is a watercolor painting,
scanner-separated and reproduced in full color.

for F.K.H. and C.W.H.
T · J

to Mom and Dad
B · D · S

Grandpa was as big around as a kettledrum. His voice was as deep as a kettledrum. When he laughed, everything near him shook like a train was passing through. And everyone else laughed too.

Grandpa lived with Grandma in a little house in the city.

He loved nothing better than a good song. Grandma said he sang so loud, the house hopped like a cricket and the pictures jumped on the walls.

"Your grandma is a lucky woman," said Grandpa. "Never does a bit of housework. Just straightens pictures all day."

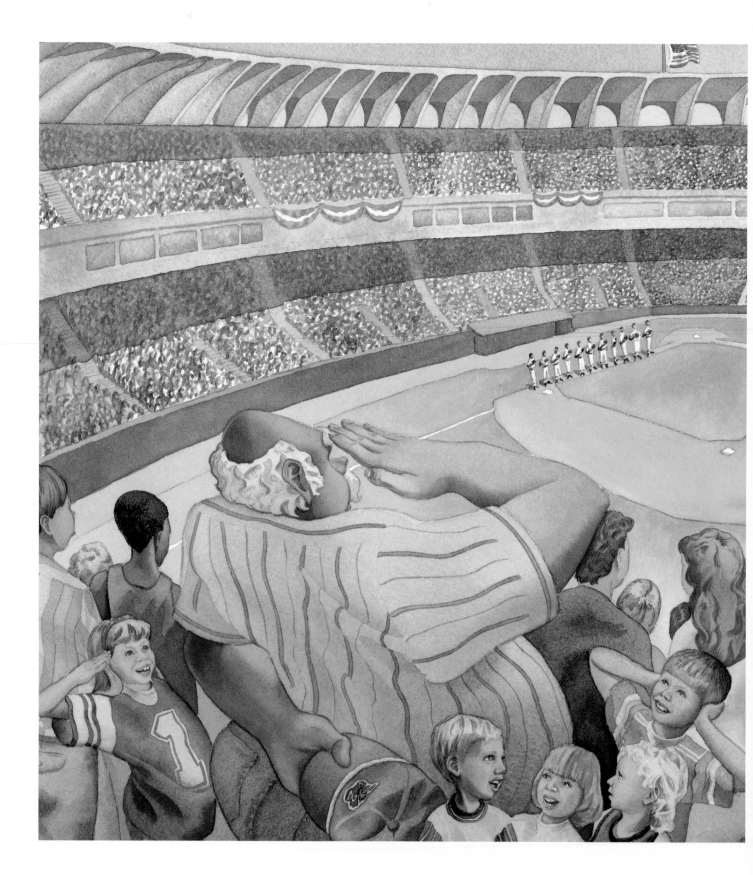

Sometimes Grandpa took us to a baseball game. He loved to salute the flag and roar out "The Star-Spangled Banner."

Sometimes he sang cowboy songs on the porch at night.
He hollered "Red River Valley" with a wolf-howl in his voice.

Sometimes he took us to the ice cream parlor. He chanted, "I scream! You scream! We all scream for ice cream!" till the pictures there shook on the walls. When a lady straightened them, he chuckled. She reminded him of Grandma.

One evening Grandpa was turning round and round by the fire, toasting himself like a marshmallow. His eyebrows were almost touching, he was thinking so hard.

"What are you thinking?" I asked.

"Really want to know?"

"Yes."

"Well, to tell the truth, I'm thinking about the best song in the world."

"What's the best song, Grandpa?"

"*Really* want to know?"

"I really do!"

"Then gather round, everyone," he said. "I can see I'll have no peace till the secret's out."

Most kids would have crowded up close for such a show. But not us.

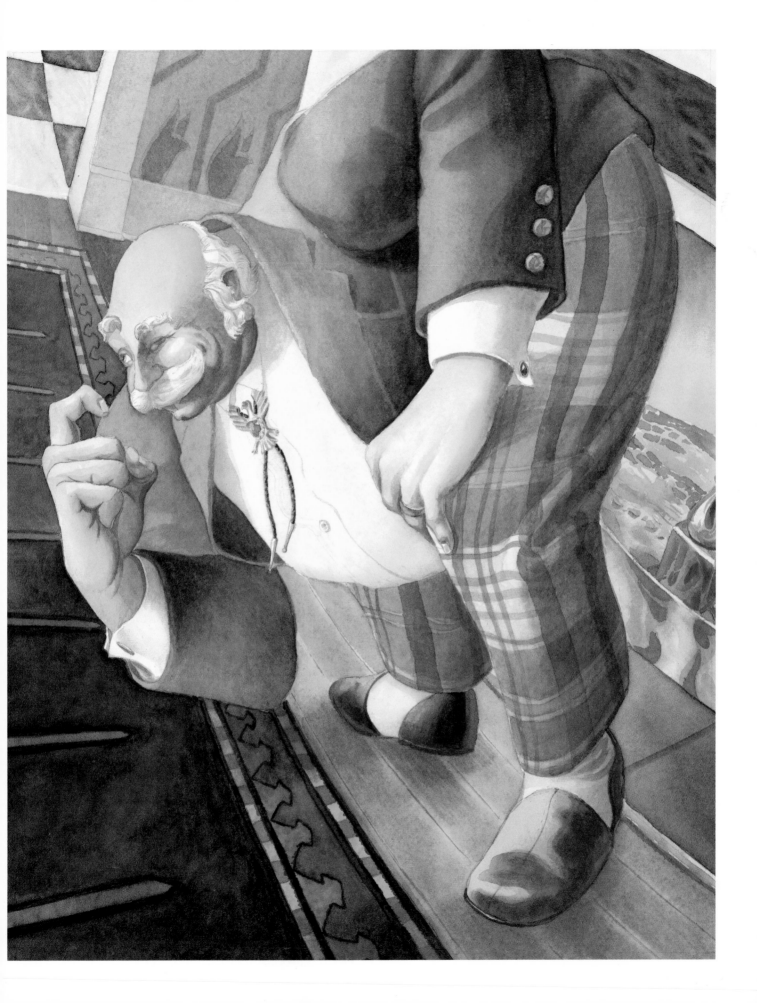

We knew it was going to be loud. So we moved way back.

Grandpa spread his feet apart and took up his singing stance.

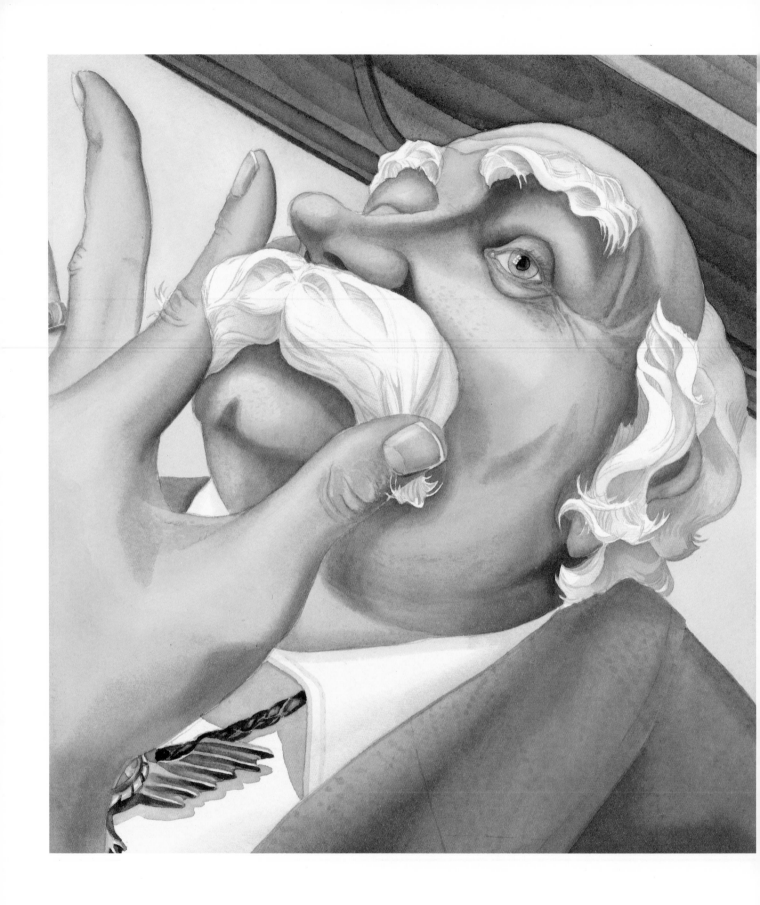

He smoothed his mustache.

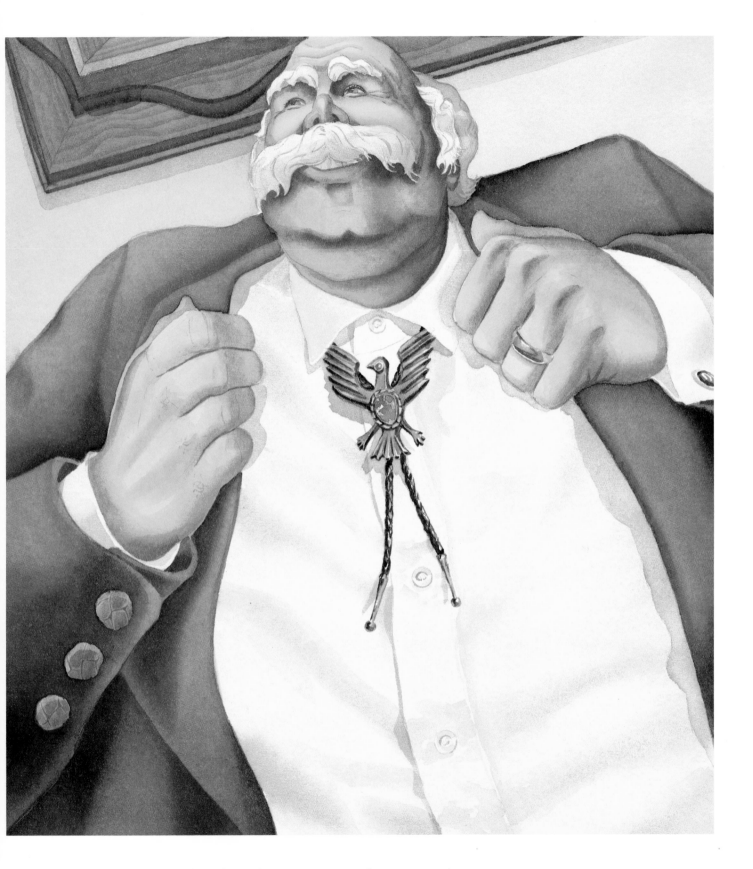

He grasped his lapels. We waited. It was so quiet you could almost hear the stars twinkling. Then...

"Hold it," Grandpa said. "Better get your grandma for this one. It's such a secret song, even *she* hasn't heard it."

Grandma stood back farthest of all, next to a picture of geese flying over the sea. Her favorite. She planned to save it if the song got too loud.

"Ready?" asked Grandpa.

"Ready!" we whooped.

So he rang out sweet as a big-bellied bell:

> *Sweet is the voice of Grandpa,*
> *Sweet as chocolate cake.*
> *True are the notes he reaches*
> *And deep as a bellyache.*
> *I love to watch his mustache*
> *Flapping like a sheet*
> *When Grandpa shakes the house down*
> *With his voice so sweet.*

Then he roared with laughter. Everything shook like a train was passing through. We laughed till we were limp. Grandma grabbed the geese, and she laughed too.

"Wherever did you get that song?" she asked.

"Made it up," Grandpa said. "And everyone has to learn it because it's the best song in the world."

So everyone learned it, then and there.

One summer day Grandpa loaded us into his old car. He started the motor, and the passengers jiggled like jelly. I sat next to him and plugged my ears—in case he started singing.

Sure enough, we rumbled downtown with the top down so a certain song he loved would not be muffled inside:

> *O, give me a home*
> *Where the buffalo roam!*

We bellowed like buffalo. Going downtown.

When we stopped—*ka-put-put-pum*—Grandpa said, "Everybody out." So we charged into the ice cream parlor.

Inside, it was as pink and white as peppermint sticks. Everything smelled sweet.

A lady in pink sailed up, starchy as a little sailboat. Grandpa boomed out:

"I scream! You scream!

We all scream—"

Then he stopped. He looked puzzled, like he'd forgotten the rest. So we yelled, "for ice cream!" and finished for him.

"Are you all right, Grandpa?" I asked.

"I've been feeling fuzzy lately. I forget things I should know. They just slip away," Grandpa said. "Must be getting old."

"You're not so old," I said.

"Then maybe it's the ice cream fumes."

He tried to laugh. But I could tell he was sad.

One night Grandpa and I were sitting on the porch. An owl flew from one tree to another, right through all the stars.

"It's pretty quiet, Grandpa," I said.

"What can we do about it?" he asked, his face as bright as the moon.

"We could sing."

Grandpa warmed up to that idea.

"Which song?" he asked, roaring up and down the scales.

"Let's sing the best song in the world."

Grandpa looked puzzled.

"You'll have to help me with that," he said quietly. "It's slipped away from me."

We held hands. I sang a line. Then he sang the line. I sang. And he sang. We sang the best song in the world.

Grandpa's birthday was coming. Grandma made plans. But Grandpa said he'd rather skip it this year.

"All that singing makes the house crooked," he said. "Wears you out straightening things."

We knew Grandpa was worried. What if he forgot the songs? What if he seemed fuzzy and old?

Then I had an idea. If we sang to him first, he wouldn't have a chance to forget.

On Grandpa's birthday the whole family came to surprise him. He was sitting by the fire in his favorite chair.

We tiptoed up and said, "Happy birthday, Grandpa."

Then we circled round him, feet apart, and took up our singing stances. We grasped our lapels (or whatever was handy) and rolled like thunder:

> *Sweet is the voice of Grandpa,*
> *Sweet as chocolate cake.*
> *True are the notes he reaches*
> *And deep as a bellyache.*
> *I love to watch his mustache*
> *Flapping like a sheet*
> *When Grandpa shakes the house down*
> *With his voice so sweet.*

We laughed till we were limp. Grandpa laughed loudest. All that caterwauling had helped him remember.

Other songs came back to him. We sang them in our sweetest voices. Of course, Grandpa's was sweetest of all.

He was really building up steam now.

He said, "That song about my sweet voice is first class. Let's sing it again."

So we sang it till everything shook.
Grandma brought a cake. It had a big crack down the middle.
"That song is a danger," she said. "A real cake-cracker."
"And to think I almost forgot it," said Grandpa.
"How could you?" I asked. "It's the best song in the world."